Squirrel's New Year's Resolution

Pat Miller

Illustrated by
Kathi Ember

Albert Whitman & Company, Chicago, Illinois

For Baby D.
Grandbaby to be.
PM

To my wonderful "family" of friends. Thanks for all your help.
I resolve to return the favor.
Love, Kathi

Library of Congress Cataloging-in-Publication Data
Miller, Pat, 1951 May 28-
Squirrel's New Year's resolution / by Pat Miller ; illustrated by Kathi Ember.
p. cm.
Summary: Squirrel cannot think of a New Year's resolution
until she realizes that by helping her friends, she has made one after all.
ISBN 978-0-8075-7591-8
[1. New Year—Fiction. 2. Helpfulness—Fiction. 3. Conduct of life—Fiction.
4. Squirrels—Fiction. 5. Forest animals—Fiction.] I. Ember, Kathi, ill. II. Title.
PZ7.M63223Sq 2010 [E]—dc22 2009049305

The artwork for this book was rendered traditionally using acrylics.

The design is by Lindaanne Donohoe.

For more information about Albert Whitman & Company,
visit our web site at www.albertwhitman.com.

S quirrel pinned up her brand new Nut-of-the-Month calendar. "It's January first," the radio said. "A great day to make a resolution."

"Make a resolution?" wondered Squirrel. "How do you do that? Bear might know." She went to see Bear at the Lonewood Library.

"Happy New Year!" he said.

"Same to you, Bear. Do you know how to make a resolution? Is it like making a snack?"

Bear laughed. "Resolutions are more important than snacks."

"More important than snacks?" said Squirrel. "What *is* a resolution?"

"A resolution is a promise you make to yourself to be better or to help others," Bear said. "When we begin a new year, we make a fresh start."

"Wow. Did *you* make a resolution?" asked Squirrel.

"I did," Bear answered. "I resolved to teach others how to read. I'm going to teach Skunk as soon as she gets well."

"Oh, no, Skunk is still sick," Squirrel thought, as she hurried to Skunk's house for a visit. She forgot all about making a resolution.

Skunk was sick of being sick.

"I'm stuck in bed until Dr. Owl says I'm better," said Skunk. "I would rather be learning to read. That's my New Year's resolution."

Squirrel knew how to cheer up her friend. She hid at the foot of the bed. She popped up and shouted, "Boo!"

Skunk giggled. Hide-and-skunk was her favorite game. Squirrel popped up again. "Boo!"

And again. "Boo!" By now Skunk was laughing hard.

Just then Dr. Owl came by. "Skunk, I can tell by your
laughter that you are feeling much better," he said, "Now you
can visit Bear. Just make sure you have a healthy lunch first."

"Lunch!" thought Squirrel. She headed toward the Hidey Hole Diner. "Maybe someone there can help me with my resolution."

On her way she met Mole and Turtle. Mole was holding a map close to his nose.

"What are you doing?' asked Squirrel.

"Turtle and I resolved to plant a garden," said Mole. "But I can't find a good place to dig with all these trees."

"Wait here," said Squirrel. She dashed up an oak tree and looked down. She spied Wildcat Creek and on its bank, a perfect place for a garden.

Squirrel scampered down and led Mole and Turtle through the woods to the edge of the creek. She helped them stake out string for the borders of the garden.

"Thanks, Squirrel. I will start digging right after lunch," said Mole.

"Lunch!" thought Squirrel, and she rushed away.
She still hadn't thought of a resolution.

At the diner, Squirrel chose a stool next to
Porcupine. He looked grumpy.

"What's wrong?" asked Squirrel.

"I resolved to be less grumpy. So I'm trying to
laugh more. But I can't think of anything funny."

"I can help you think of something funny. Like, why did the squirrel run back and forth across the road?"

"I don't know, why?" asked Porcupine.

"Because she was nuts!" laughed Squirrel.

Porcupine laughed, too. "I get it! That reminds me. What's striped and bouncy?"

"Tell me," giggled Squirrel.

"Skunk on a trampoline!" said Porcupine. Squirrel laughed herself right off the stool.

Porcupine said, "That's a good one! I'd better write these down." Off he went to find paper and pencil.

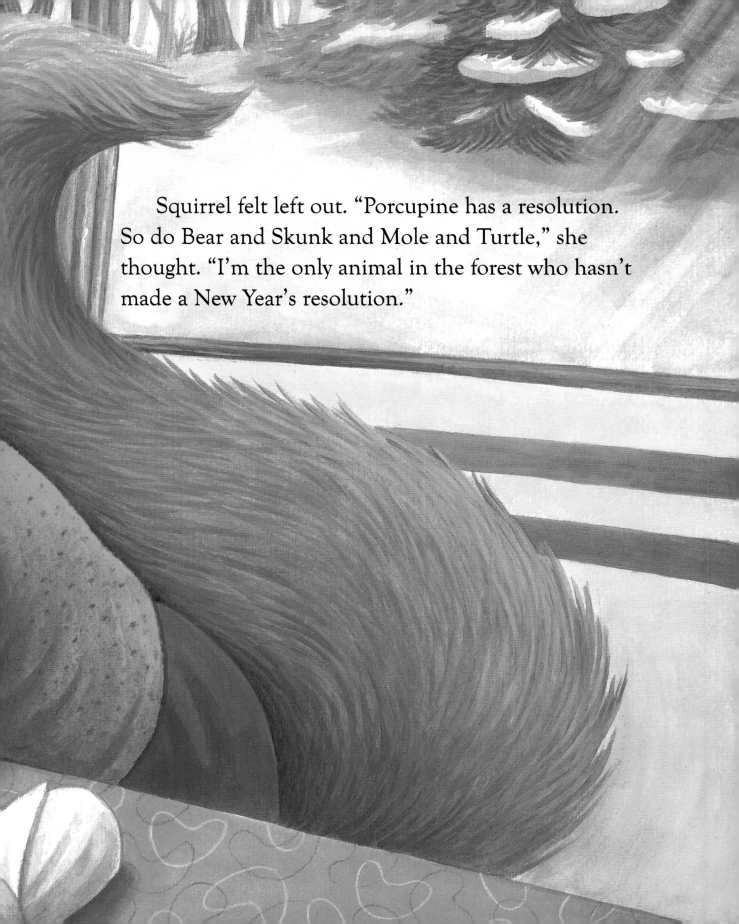

Squirrel felt left out. "Porcupine has a resolution. So do Bear and Skunk and Mole and Turtle," she thought. "I'm the only animal in the forest who hasn't made a New Year's resolution."

Rabbit came to take Squirrel's order. "Would you like to try my New Year's Special?" asked Rabbit.

"Sure," said Squirrel. "Maybe it will help me make a resolution. I wish I knew how."

"Think of a way to improve yourself. Or a way to use what you're good at to help others," said Rabbit.

Squirrel ate her lunch special and thought hard.

Just then, Skunk came in. "I need a healthy
lunch! Thanks to Squirrel, I'm feeling better!"
"Sit with me, Skunk," Bear called. "I see you
brought our first book."

Turtle and Mole came in next. "What do you
have for two thirsty animals who just started a garden?"
said Mole.

"Squirrel found a terrific place for it," said Turtle.

Porcupine hurried in. "Do you
know why Bear said 'Caw, caw?'"

Before anyone could answer, Porcupine
said, "He was learning another language!"
All the animals laughed.

"I didn't know you were so funny," said Mole.

"Me, either," said Porcupine. "Squirrel got
me started."

Rabbit said to Squirrel, "You're doing a good job on your resolution."

"I didn't know I had one," said Squirrel.

"Your actions are better than words. It looks like you resolved to help someone every day," said Rabbit.

"Really?" asked Squirrel. "I did it! I made my
very first resolution!"
"Hurray for Squirrel!" shouted all the animals.

It was going to be a very happy New Year.